ALFIE

SLIDES INTO WINTER

Maggie Holden

MAPLE
PUBLISHERS

Alfie Slides into Winter

Author: Maggie Holden

Illustrations by Denis Stapleton

Copyright © Maggie Holden (2022)

The right of Maggie Holden to be identified as author of this work has been asserted by the author in accordance with section 77 and 78 of the Copyright, Designs and Patents Act 1988.

First Published in 2022

ISBN 978-1-915796-29-5 (Paperback)

Published by:
    Maple Publishers
    Fairbourne Drive, Atterbury,
    Milton Keynes,
    MK10 9RG, UK
    www.maplepublishers.com

Book Layout by:
    White Magic Studios
    www.whitemagicstudios.co.uk

A CIP catalogue record for this title is available from the British Library.

Alfie has been growing up through all the seasons of the year.

In this book he samples the pleasures and troubles of winter.

Molly his friend who he met in previous stories is given a permanent home with him and they enjoy winter fun with other friends they had made earlier.

Alfie was three years old
On a day when his world turned white.
Looking through the window he thought
"Oh my what a pretty sight ."

But when he went outside
He quickly changed his mind
The wind blew hard, the snow was cold
And to his paws not kind.

" I think it's best inside " he thought,
"More sleep can do no harm
And perhaps much later on
The weather will be calm."

Alfie returned to his favourite spot
A cosy rug by the fire
The best place on a freezing day
For a pussycat to retire.

Later that night the cat flap creaked
And two yellow eyes shone bright
"Are you coming out to hunt
Or are you in there for the night?"

"Molly if you get caught there'll be a scene
I've told you once or twice
And I don't like this winter weather
It really isn't nice".

"There's not much to do out in the cold
Let's stay warm and dry inside.
I'm sure if we look hard enough
We'll find somewhere for you to hide".

So they crept around the house
While everyone was asleep
Until they found under the stairs
A cupboard with blankets in a heap.

"That's it Molly, snuggle down.
No one will find you here
And when dawn breaks I'll let you out
So you can go while the coast is clear".

The next morning dawned really bright
But the wind blew cold and strong.
Poor Molly shivered outside in the doorway
Hoping that winter wouldn't last long.

Alfie seeing her plight from inside
Set up a wailing song
And everyone rushed into the hallway
Gathering to see what was wrong.

The door was opened and the cold rushed in.
"Come inside "said Alfie ,"We'll look after you".
Molly obeyed as she could sense
That what Alfie said was really true.

They gave her a great big bowl of food,
They wiped and dried her fur
And as she lay on the rug by the fire
She discovered that she could purr.

Another night, then next day
The snow lay white and deep.
Alfie rushing through the flap
Slipped over in a heap.

Because over night the snow had frozen
And was now as slippery as could be.
The two friends took to the slopes
Slipping and sliding, legs swinging free.

They ventured down to the river
That was frozen in a strip
And the ducks coming into land
Found it impossible not to slip.

Then suddenly something hit Alfie -
A snowball flying free.
They heard whispering and giggling
That came from behind a tree.

Maggie Holden

Alfie scooped a paw full of snow
Then Molly did the same
And everyone was ready
To start a snowball game.

Betty, Boris, Biddy and Bob
All ready for the fun
Jumped out from behind the tree
And the excitement had begun.

"Battle stations", Alfie called
Ducking and dodging as snowballs flew
The badgers against Alfie and Molly
But that made four against two.

"We're outnumbered here", Alfie cried
"We'll never win this fight"
But just then their friends arrived
The rabbit, and the thrush up above in flight.

It was not long before everyone
Was wet and feeling tired
So a final truce was called
And the last snowball fired.

When next morning dawned
The day was still and bright
And with a gentle drip drip
The snow was melting out of sight.

Molly and Alfie went to look
At the thawing snow
And Molly climbed up in a tree
To sit and watch it go.

Alfie sitting underneath
Was not in the place to be
Because the snow came falling down
In a rush out of the tree.

Alfie sat in an unhappy heap
And Molly could not hide her delight
At the soggy, dripping, bedraggled cat
Sitting in her sight.

But nothing lasts forever
Winter soon would stop
And Spring was round the corner
With every drip and drop.

Molly and Alfie returned together
To the cottage that was their home
And cheerfully Molly would tell her tale
Now she need no longer roam.

Books in this Series:

When Monty Met Alfie

Alfie Leaps Into Spring

Alfie Splashes Into Summer

Alfie Ambles Into Autumn

Forthcoming Titles:

Molly's Tale

Alfie and Molly's Kittens Running Wild

ALFIE SLIDES
INTO WINTER

Alfie has been growing up through all the seasons of the year.

In this book he samples the pleasures and drawbacks of winter.

Molly, his friend from previous adventures is given a permanent home with him and they meet up with old friends from earlier stories.

Written in verse and humorously illustrated ALFIE SLIDES INTO WINTER will entertain cat lovers of all ages.

Lightning Source UK Ltd.
Milton Keynes UK
UKHW051919211222
414255UK00005B/19